THE VIPER

Lisa Thiesing

PUFFIN BOOKS

PUFFIN BOOKS
Published by Penguin Group
Penguin Young Readers Group, 345 Hudson St., New York, NY 10014
Penguin Books Ltd, 80 Strand, London WC2R ORL, England
Penguin Books Australia Ltd, 250 Camberwell Road, Camberwell, Victoria 3124, Australia
Penguin Books Canada Ltd, 10 Alcorn Avenue, Toronto, Ontario, Canada M4V 3B2
Penguin Books (N.Z.) Ltd, 182-190 Wairau Road, Auckland 10, New Zealand

First published in the United States of America by Dutton Children's Books,
a division of Penguin Putnam Books for Young Readers, 2002
Published by Puffin Books, a division of Penguin Young Readers Group, 2003

1   3   5   7   9   10   8   6   4   2

THE LIBRARY OF CONGRESS HAS CATALOGED THE DUTTON EDITION AS FOLLOWS:
Thiesing, Lisa
The Viper! / by Lisa Thiesing.—1st ed.
p.   cm.
Summary: Peggy receives a mysterious phone call from the Viper,
warning that he is coming in one year, with repeated calls
which count down the dwindling time until his arrival.
ISBN 0-525-46892-7
[1. Fear—Fiction. 2. Humorous stories.] I. Title.
PZ7.T35615 Vi 2002   [E]—dc21 2001047141

Puffin Easy-to-Read ISBN 0-14-250157-3
Puffin® and Easy-to-Read® are registered trademarks of Penguin Group (USA) Inc.
Designed by Ellen M. Lucaire
Manufactured in China

Reading Level 2.3

For Max—
who always protected me from vipers

On a Friday,

the phone rang.

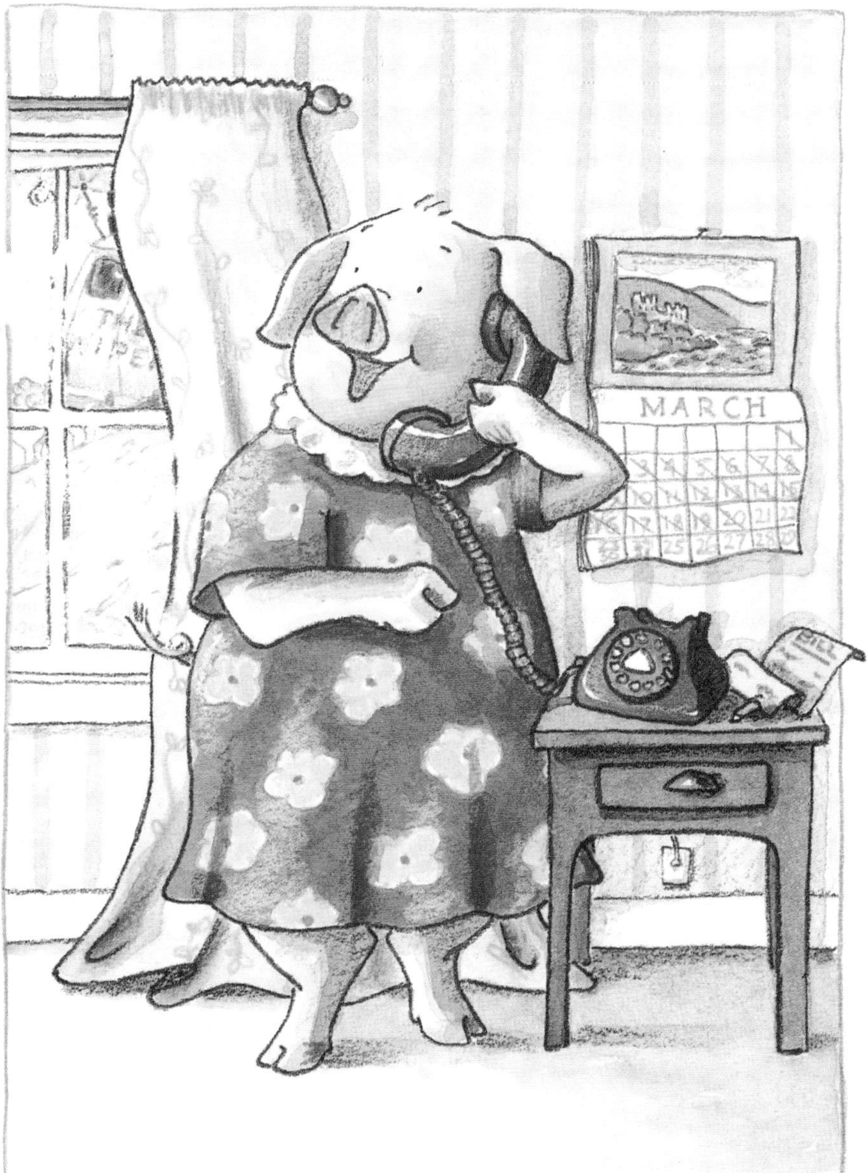
MARCH

"Hello," said Peggy.

A husky, dusky voice hissed,

"I am zee Viper.

I vill come in 1 year."

"The Viper? How odd!"

Peggy said to herself.

"1 year. Well, that's

12 whole months from now.

365 days. Not to worry."

The months passed.

All was well.

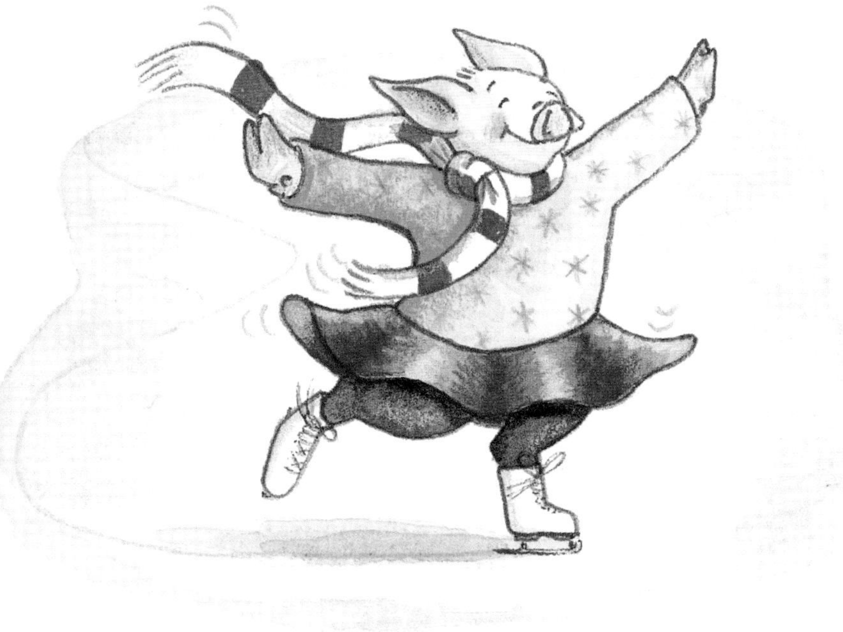

And then . . .

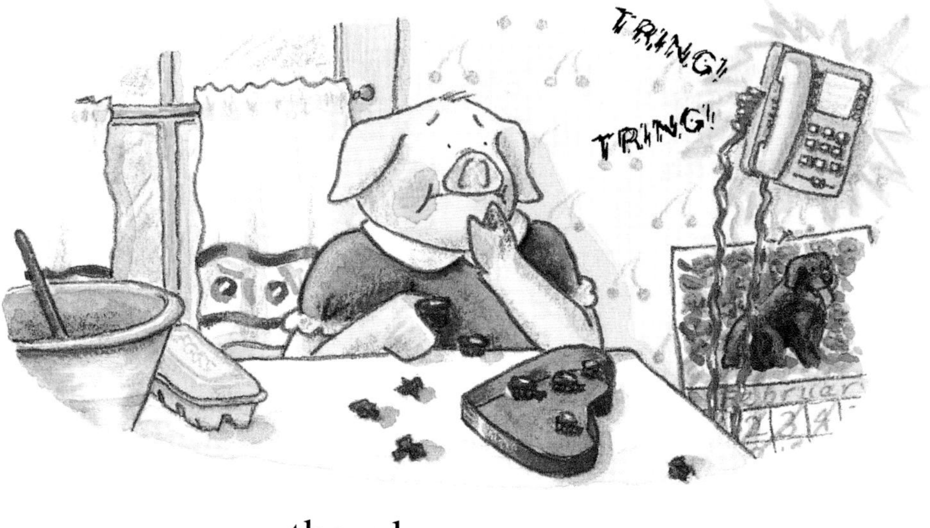
TRING!
TRING!

the phone rang.

"I am zee Viper.

I vill come in 1 month."

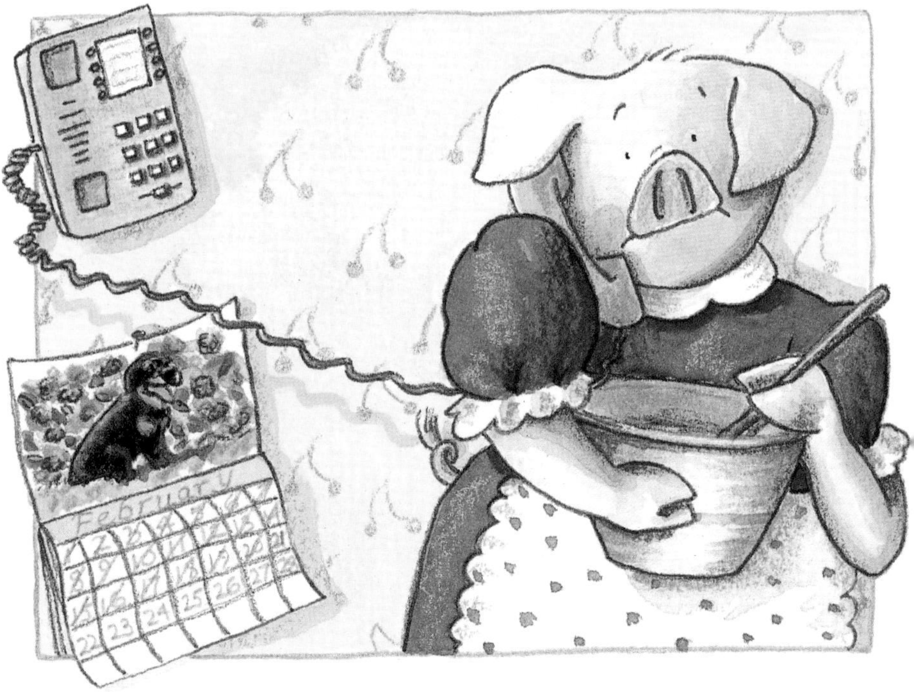
February

"Let's see,"

thought Peggy out loud.

"30 days has September,

April, June, and November."

"All the rest have 31,

except February, which has 28,

unless it's a leap year,

and then it has 29."

"What's a viper anyway,

I wonder?"

Peggy looked up the word.

"OK. Hmm.

Violet . . . violin . . .

Ah! *Viper!*

A fanged, poisonous snake!

Oh my!"

"Why in the world would

a fanged, poisonous snake

be calling me?

Oooh, I hate snakes!"

Peggy was in bed.

The phone rang.

"I am zee Viper.

I vill come in 1 veek."

Now Peggy was awake.

So she went downstairs.

"Might as well have

a little snack.

7 days to go."

Sunday, Monday, and Tuesday
were pretty quiet.

Peggy did her chores.

She had fun, too.

But on Wednesday . . .

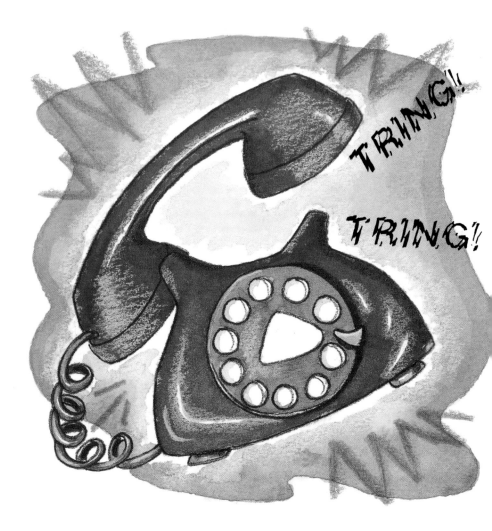

"I am zee Viper.

I vill come in 3 days."

Peggy was getting nervous.

"That's Saturday!"

On Thursday,

"I am zee Viper.

I vill come in 2 days."

On Friday,

"I am zee Viper.

I vill come in 1 day."

Then, on Saturday,

"I am zee Viper.

I vill come at

12 o'clock."

"Noon! That's only

2 hours from now.

What to do?"

Set a trap!

String garlic around your neck!

Bolt the door!

Call the cops!

At 11 o'clock,

"I am zee Viper.

I vill come in 1 hour."

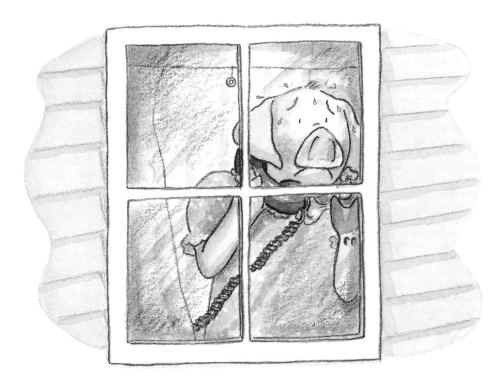

55 minutes later,

"I am zee Viper.

I vill come in 5 minutes."

4 minutes later,

"I am zee Viper.

I vill come in 1 minute."

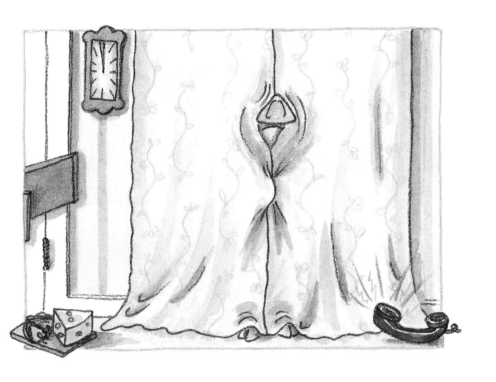

Just 60 seconds left!

Hide!

Turn out the lights!

Peggy heard the creak of the fence . . .

the rattle of chains . . .

a slithering sound . . .

something,

someone, being dragged . . .

10, 9, 8, 7, 6, 5, 4, 3, 2, 1 . . .

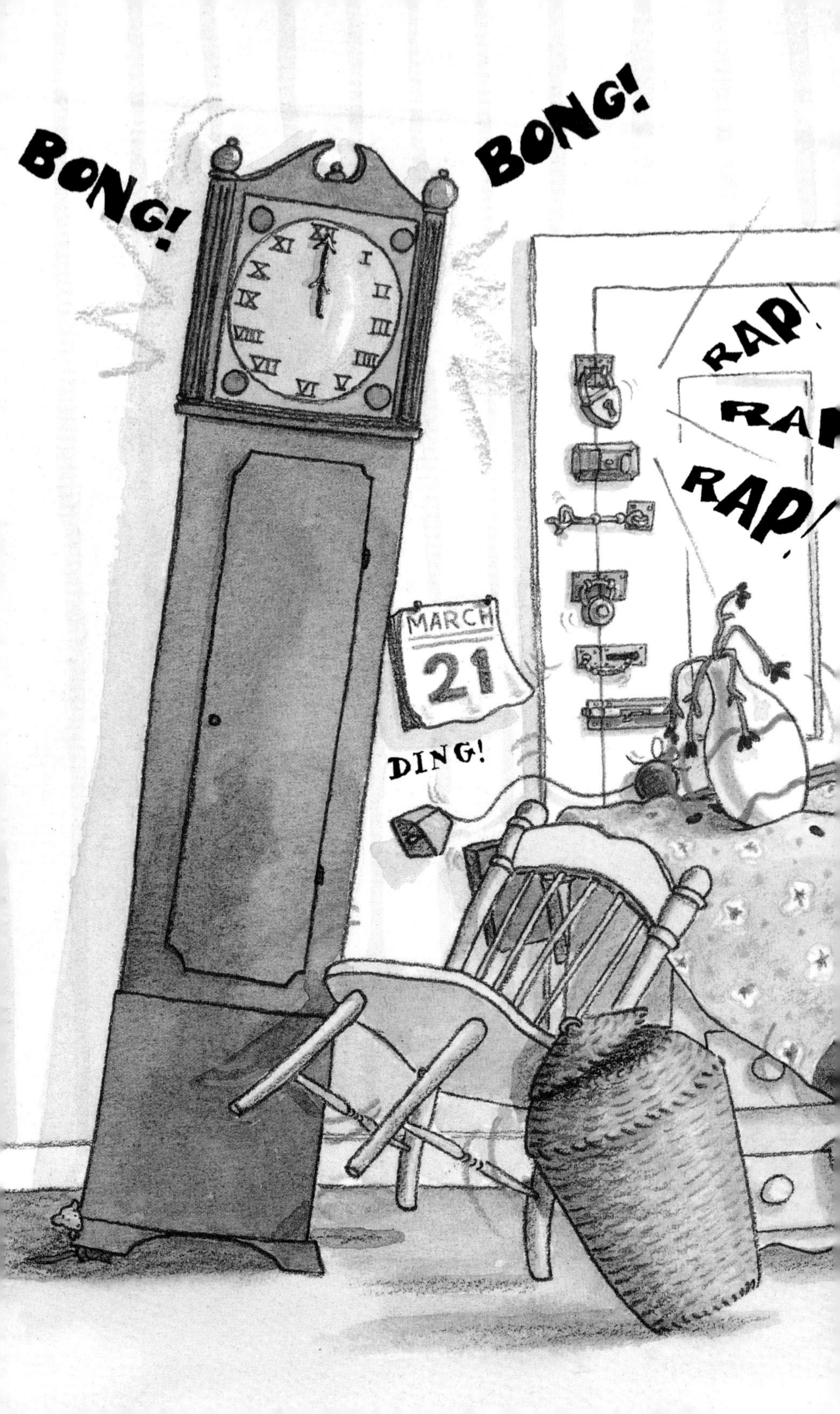
BONG!
BONG!
RAP!
RAP!
RAP!
MARCH
21
DING!

"I am zee Viper.

I am at your door!"

Look through

the peephole,

if you dare . . .

“I am zee Viper,” he said.

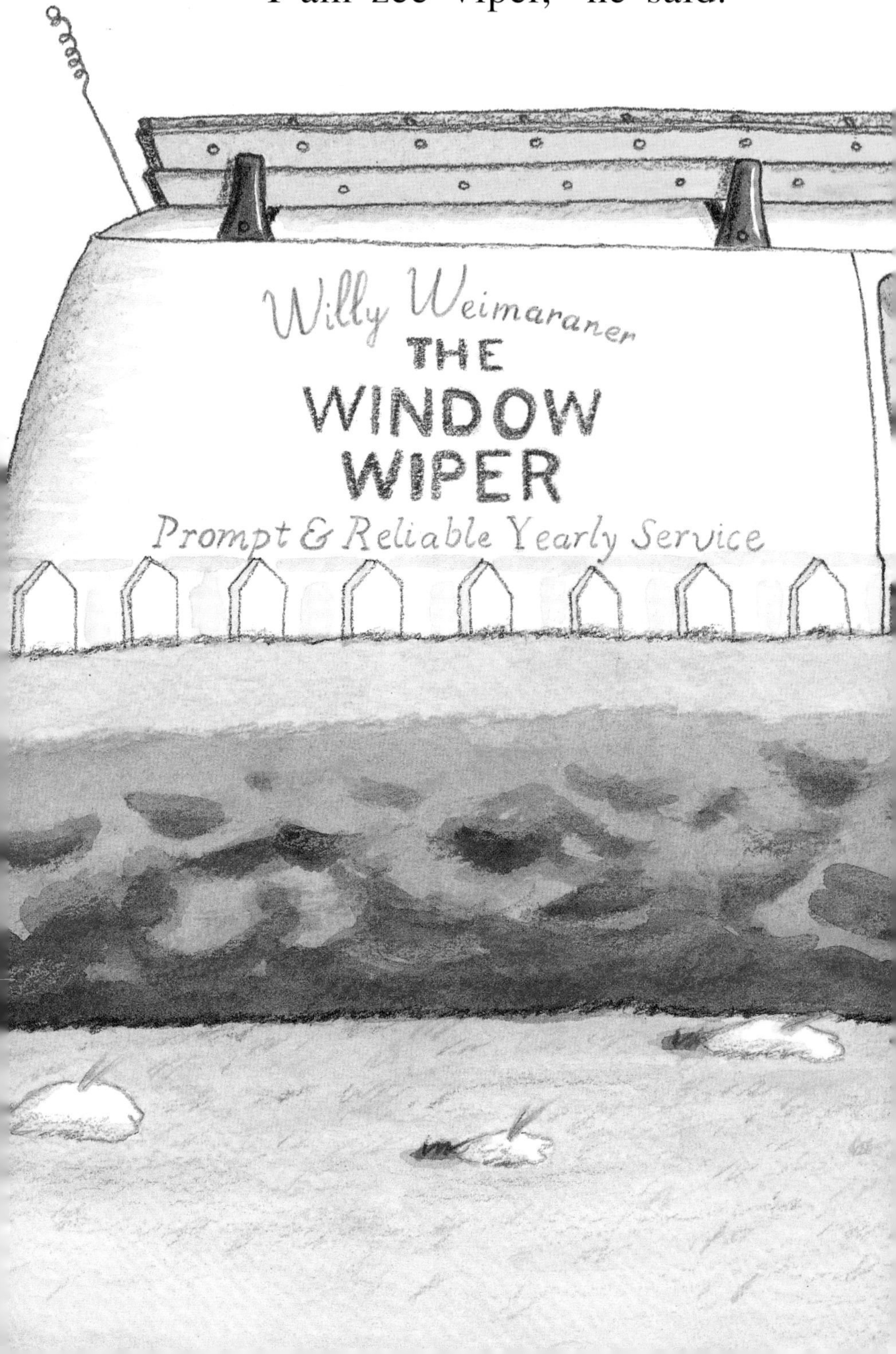
Willy Weimaraner
THE
WINDOW
WIPER
Prompt & Reliable Yearly Service

"I have come

to vipe your vindows!"

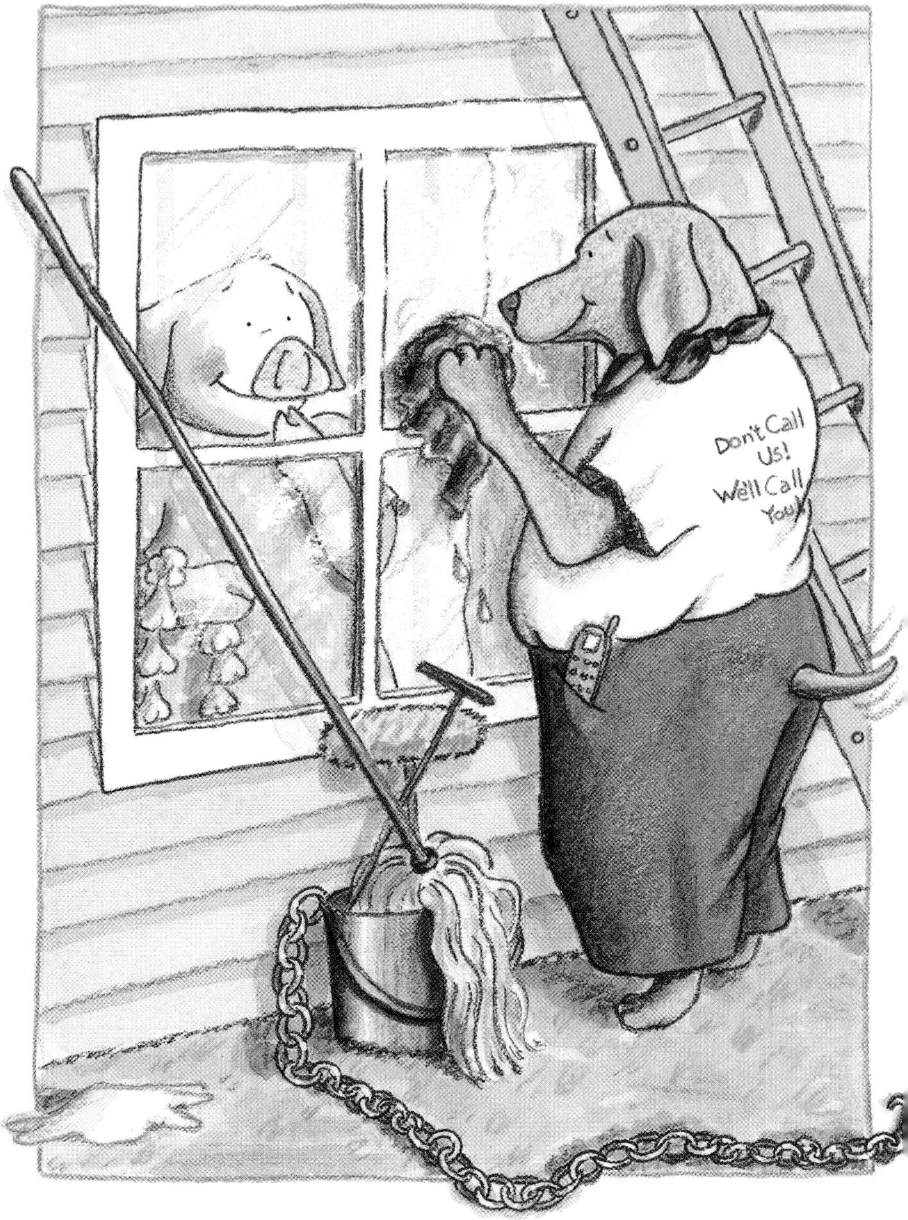
Don't Call
Us!
We'll Call
You!

And so he did.

9/1